To Ed,
my brownie prince,
and wizard,
and all that is magical in my life

MEET THE

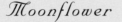

Moonflower

NAME:
Erin Young

FAIRY NAME AND SPIRIT:
Moonflower

WAND:
Enchanted Icicle that
Never Melts

GIFT:
Ability to motivate and
inspire others

MENTOR:
Grandmother,
Madam Mariposa

Rosemary

NAME:
Bailey Richardson

FAIRY NAME AND SPIRIT:
Rosemary

WAND:
Nine Strands of Orangutan Hair,
Triple Braided

GIFT:
An amazing memory

MENTOR:
Mrs. Clark,
Madam Chameleon

Moonflower

and

the Pearl of Paramour

J. H. Sweet

Illustrated by Holly Sierra

SOURCEBOOKS
Jabberwocky
AN IMPRINT OF SOURCEBOOKS

Published by Sourcebooks Jabberwocky, an imprint of Sourcebooks, Inc.
P.O. Box 4410, Naperville, Illinois 60567-4410
(630) 961-3900
Fax: (630) 961-2168
www.sourcebooks.com

Library of Congress Cataloging-in-Publication Data

Sweet, J. H.
    Moonflower and the Pearl of Paramour / J.H. Sweet.
        p. cm. — (The fairy chronicles ; bk. 12)
    Summary: After a powerful wizard casts a spell separating two young lovers from each other by trapping them in a painting and a book, Moonflower and her fairy friends embark on a mission to free them.
    [1. Fairies—Fiction. 2. Love—Fiction. 3. Magic—Fiction.] I. Title.
    PZ7.S9547Mo 2008
    [Fic]—dc22

                        2008002787

                Printed and bound in China.
                OGP 10 9 8 7 6 5 4 3 2 1

FAIRY TEAM

Primrose

NAME:
Taylor Buchanan

FAIRY NAME AND SPIRIT:
Primrose

WAND:
Small, Black Raven Feather

GIFT:
Ability to solve mysteries

MENTOR:
Mrs. Renquist,
Madam Swallowtail

Luna

NAME:
Hope Valdez

FAIRY NAME AND SPIRIT:
Luna

WAND:
Single Thorn from
Prickly Pear Cactus

GIFT:
Strength, endurance,
and ability to perform magic
without a wand

MENTOR:
Amelia Thompson,
Madam Finch

Inside you is the power to do anything™

Marigold and the Feather of Hope, the Journey Begins
Dragonfly and the Web of Dreams
Thistle and the Shell of Laughter
Firefly and the Quest of the Black Squirrel
Spiderwort and the Princess of Haiku
Periwinkle and the Cave of Courage
Cinnabar and the Island of Shadows
Mimosa and the River of Wisdom
Primrose and the Magic Snowglobe
Luna and the Well of Secrets
Dewberry and the Lost Chest of Paragon
Moonflower and the Pearl of Paramour
Snapdragon and the Odyssey of Élan
Harlequin and the Pebble of Spree

Come visit us at fairychronicles.com

$\mathscr{C}$ontents

Chapter One: Moonflower. 1

Chapter Two: Fairy Circle 14

Chapter Three: Concerning Brownies. 21

Chapter Four: Henry and Rose. 30

Chapter Five: The Wishing Star 40

Chapter Six: Paramour and the
Pearl of Love 60

Chapter Seven: The Candle of
Inamorata. 73

Chapter Eight: Castle Penchaant and
the Twisted Staircase. 83

Fairy Fun 100

Fairy Facts 104

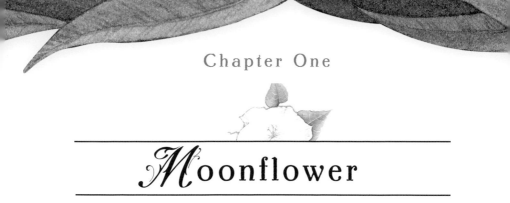

Chapter One

Moonflower

Early morning on Valentine's Day, Erin Young was setting out materials for valentine making. Erin was staying the weekend at her grandmother's house because her parents were vacationing at a bed and breakfast for their anniversary.

This year, Valentine's Day fell on a Saturday, which was perfect. In about an hour, Erin's friend, Bailey Richardson, was due to arrive for a two-night sleepover. This was also a three-day weekend because Monday was President's Day, so the girls would have plenty of time for their planned activities.

Erin carefully laid out the ribbons, paper punches, stencils, fancy stationery, glitter, rubber stamps, glue, and markers for making valentines. The girls were also planning to make several friendship bracelets as gifts, so Erin got out embroidery floss in various colors and an assortment of tiny beads.

Later in the afternoon, the girls would be attending a special celebration, during which they would exchange the valentine and bracelet creations.

Having moved from Kentucky to Texas the previous year, Erin was especially happy to have made a friend like Bailey. Erin had just turned ten years old in January, and Bailey was nearly eleven. Even though Bailey was a year older, the girls had a lot in common because in addition to being just like regular girls, they were also fairies. This meant that they had each been given a fairy spirit.

Blessed with a moonflower fairy spirit, Erin was known as Moonflower to other fairies. Standard fairy form was six inches high. In fairy form, Moonflower wore a creamy white dress made of softly glowing moonflower petals. Her pointy, pearly-white slippers matched her dress, and she had tall, fringed, milky-white wings. She also wore a moonflower hairclip to pull back her long, curly brown hair.

In the belt of her dress Moonflower carried a small pouch of pixie dust, the fairy handbook, and her wand, which was an enchanted icicle that would never melt. The icicle glinted and shone in the light like a beautiful crystal prism.

Pixie dust was glittering magical dust provided for the fairies by Mother Nature and used for various purposes. And the fairy handbook contained answers to fairy questions, along with information and advice to help fairies make wise decisions.

It was a valuable tool for young fairies and had the ability to age with them. Right now, Moonflower's handbook gave answers to questions that a ten-year-old would understand. As she grew older, and needed more information, the handbook would give more detailed explanations of the sort that a maturing fairy would find useful. Moonflower's handbook was a soft, pale green color, which was different than those of the Texas fairies. This was because it had originated in Kentucky. Most of the Texas fairies carried handbooks of a fawn tan color.

Sometimes fairy spirits ran in families. Moonflower's younger sister, Darlene, was also a fairy. Darlene was eight and was blessed with the fairy spirit of a teasel plant, which was both an herb and a wildflower.

Each young fairy was assigned a mentor fairy as a supervisor. This was necessary

Moonflower

because it was a huge responsibility to be a fairy. Fairies had the important job of protecting nature and fixing serious problems. No fairy was ever allowed to use magic for trivial things or to abuse others.

Moonflower's mentor was none other than her grandmother who was looking after her for the weekend. Eunice Young was blessed with a mariposa butterfly fairy spirit and was known as Madam Mariposa to other fairies. In fairy form, she wore a silky, dark gray dress that came almost to her ankles. Her magnificent velvety wings were also gray with yellow and orange accents. Madam Mariposa's wand was a single, frosted-purple hawthorn berry that dangled from its dark brown stem like a hanging lantern.

Moonflower was one of the rarest fairies in existence. In fact, the moonflower fairy spirit was every bit as rare as the elusive edelweiss fairy spirit of Austria. Madam

Toad, leader of the fairies for the Southwest region, had done some research and had discovered that there was only one moonflower fairy in all of North America, as far as anyone knew.

Each fairy was given a special fairy gift relating to her fairy spirit. Moonflower's gift was the ability to motivate and inspire others. She was also a master storyteller. Her gift was still developing and in the future would expand to include the ability to inspire love and passion because the moonflower was a flower of passion. The petals of the moonflower were commonly used in love potions concocted by witches and wizards. Moonflower's gifts were especially potent after dark because moonflowers only opened at night. Madam Mariposa had been given the special gift of strength and endurance that was common to all butterfly and moth fairies.

Bailey arrived at seven-thirty with her bag for the sleepover. Her fairy spirit came from the rosemary herb. As a fairy, Rosemary wore a frosty green dress made of spiky rosemary leaves with tiny, pale blue flowers scattered over it. She also had small, misty green wings, and her light brown hair was short and wavy. Rosemary was the most fragrant of all the fairies and smelled like pine trees and mint mixed together. She carried a wand made of nine braided orangutan hairs, and her special fairy gift was an amazing memory. Rosemary never forgot a name, and she didn't have to study as hard in school as many of her friends because she could remember things very easily. She could often recite long passages from books, word for word, after only a single read through.

Rosemary was glad to get away from home for a couple of days. Two brownies lived with the Richardson family. Brownies were boy fairies, about seven inches high, and they were very mischievous. They delighted in playing tricks and pranks. When brownies lived in regular people's houses, they could be very helpful with things like untangling thread, cleaning out grass from under lawnmowers, organizing kitchen drawers, and fishing out socks from behind the dryer. However, if not rewarded properly with plenty of milk and pastries, their mischief could get out of control very quickly.

Ryan and Edgar had lived with Rosemary's family for nearly two years. However, Rosemary's parents did not know there were brownies living in their house because regular people could not recognize fairies and brownies. If non-magical people happened to see them, fairies and brownies would only look like their fairy spirits of flowers, butterflies, plants, acorns, birds, insects, stones, and such like. Brownies derived their spirits from earthy things like pinecones, mosses, river stones, and mushrooms.

But it was in the brownies' nature to cause trouble, so Rosemary kept very busy. In fact, only the night before, she had spent nearly an hour straightening up her mother's sewing cabinet because Ryan and Edgar had tangled, twisted, and tossed nearly every item while rooting through the cabinet and playing with things.

The brownies told Rosemary that they were going to straighten it all out in the morning. However, Rosemary knew that her mother was planning to hem a skirt and would likely discover the mess before Ryan and Edgar had a chance to clean it up.

Before leaving for the sleepover, Rosemary had put out half a cherry turnover and some milk for the boys. She had also encouraged them to keep their pranks under control while she was gone, or maybe go on a few outings with their bird and animal friends.

Brownies had a special relationship with many animals and birds, and had a deep respect for them. Since brownies couldn't fly, they rode on birds and animals to travel. Similarly, brownies were very helpful to their furred and feathered friends whenever possible, so they basically had a partnership with them.

As Rosemary and Moonflower were making valentines and friendship bracelets, they received a nut message from another fairy friend. The message was from Beth who was a marigold fairy. In the note, Marigold told them that there would be three new fairies at Fairy Circle that afternoon: a blue dragonfly fairy, a cricket fairy, and a dove fairy.

Fairy Circles were gatherings of fairies for the purposes of celebration and discussion

of serious problems and ways to fix them. At the end of nearly every Fairy Circle, several select fairies were dispatched on an adventure to solve a particular problem. Under the careful guidance and leadership of Madam Toad, the fairies of the Southwest region had never failed on a mission.

Since fairy activities had to be kept secret from regular people, fairy mentors usually arranged excuses or activities such as sleepovers so that the young fairies could participate in fairy adventures.

After a delicious lunch of salad, pepperoni pizza, and root beer, which were some of the fairies' favorite foods, Madam Mariposa loaded the girls into her car with their valentines and bracelets. They all buckled up and set off to a secluded park on the outskirts of town.

Chapter Two

Fairy Circle

oday the fairies were meeting under a beautiful apricot tree, which had just decided to bloom early for spring. Madam Toad always chose the site for Fairy Circle very carefully. Since this was Valentine's Day, the fairy leader had chosen an apricot tree because apricot trees were symbolic of love. The lower branches of the tree had been decorated with dangling paper hearts that were enchanted to glow softly and play musical notes. The simple songs sounded much like tunes played by tinkling wind chimes.

Moonflower and Rosemary visited with many of their fairy friends including Tulip, Pumpkinwing, Lily, Cinnabar, Firefly, Snapdragon, Luna, Primrose, and Hollyhock.

Primrose was interpreting in sign language for her cousin, Hollyhock, who was the only deaf fairy in their group.

However, many of the young fairies were learning American Sign Language, so Primrose didn't have to work very hard. Hollyhock could also read lips very well and often didn't need an interpreter at all.

A young fairy named Kayla, whose spirit was that of a dustywing skipper butterfly, was letting the other fairies know that she now preferred to be known as Dusty, instead of Skipper, as she had been called before. This was fine with everyone, since fairies were free to choose any name they pleased. Skipper had decided that since she had grown up some, Dusty sounded a little more like an older fairy; and the difference between seven and eight years old could sometimes be great.

Dusty's sister, Rachel, was a morning glory fairy. She was traveling around Fairy Circle with her sister, letting her friends know, "But I still want to be called Morning Glory."

The blue dragonfly fairy had arrived and was now surrounded by other fairies anxious to meet her. Since the Southwest region already had a red dragonfly fairy known as Dragonfly, the blue dragonfly fairy informed the group that she would like to be called Blue.

While talking to her, Dragonfly discovered that Blue's special fairy gift involved incredible swimming and diving abilities because dragonflies were born in the water. Blue was a fantastic swimmer and diver, and was also on a junior water polo team. She was also hoping someday to get a swimming scholarship to a college.

In contrast, Dragonfly's special gift was speed and coordination. She was very good at soccer because she was so fast and agile. She liked to swim too, like all dragonfly fairies, but water abilities seemed to be specific to Blue as a fairy gift.

Madam Mariposa

By the time most of the fairies had had a chance to talk to Blue, the dove and cricket fairies had arrived.

Moonflower discovered that Dove's special fairy gift was the ability to settle conflicts and promote peace. She could also inspire pleasant dreams because good dreams were often delivered to mankind on the wings of doves.

Cricket had exceptional musical abilities. She could sing beautifully and bewitchingly, and was in the choir both at school and at her church. Cricket could also play piano well and was often able to play songs after just hearing them, without having to use sheet music. Her fairy gifts were still developing, just like Moonflower's. Cricket had discovered over Christmas that she also had the ability to cause rain, though she didn't yet understand how to control this power, and had not yet figured out the exact instances in which it could or should be used.

The fairies all happily visited with their new friends, while they exchanged valentines and friendship bracelets and helped to lay out refreshments brought by Madam Chameleon and Madam Monarch.

They had their usual fairy fare of peanut butter and marshmallow crème sandwiches, raspberries, powdered sugar puff pastries, lemon jellybeans, and homemade fudge; but today, they also enjoyed special frosted valentine cookies and fluffy coconut cake. And there were a variety of drinks to choose from including pomegranate juice, hot chocolate, ginger ale, and root beer.

As the fairies were enjoying the treats, two brownies arrived at the Fairy Circle meeting, riding on a large golden eagle.

Chapter Three

Concerning
Brownies...

rownie Christopher, leader of the brownies, was one of the visitors. He had been blessed with an acorn brownie spirit and was dressed all in tan with an acorn cap for a hat. At age fifteen, Christopher was slightly older than a lot of brownies in the area and had been brownie leader for three years. His companion's name was Jeffrey, also age fifteen. He too was dressed in tan but wore a cinnamon-colored vest and shoes. Jeffrey was a river stone brownie and wore a string of polished gray, black, and brown river stones around his neck. Christopher had dark brown hair, while Jeffrey's hair was sandy blond.

Moonflower and Rosemary presented Christopher and Jeffrey with dark red friendship bracelets. The girls had purposely made extra bracelets in anticipation of giving them to Fairy Circle visitors. The brownies were surprised and somewhat embarrassed to receive the valentine gifts. They blushed a little and quietly thanked the fairies. But they must have liked the presents because both boys put the bracelets on their wrists right away.

Some of the fairies were getting restless waiting for the meeting to begin. Madam Toad was talking to Madam June Beetle and Madam Finch. It was rumored that in January, Madam Toad had had an in-person meeting with Mother Nature over some mysterious and terrible problem with a young fairy named Dewberry. The other young fairies wondered about this and

were much in awe that Madam Toad was brave enough to meet with Mother Nature directly.

Mother Nature was the guardian of fairies and all other magical creatures. She was also the supervisor of nature and could take any form of nature. Mother Nature was often in dangerous forms such as earthquake, geyser, quicksand, and hailstorm. No one could ever predict when she would take a safe form like drizzle, echo, morning dew, or rainbow.

Madam Toad introduced the brownies as she called the meeting to order. "Brownie Christopher and Brownie Jeffrey need our help to accomplish a very important mission. Please give them your full attention while they explain the situation." With this, she turned the meeting over to Christopher.

Christopher had attended several Fairy Circle gatherings before and was comfortable in speaking to the group. He began with, "It is true. The brownies once again need your help. But before I tell you about the task, I want to explain a few things about brownies.

"Many people don't know that brownies, in addition to having brownie spirits, are also regular boys just like fairies are regular girls. What is different about brownies is that most are orphans. The reason orphans, rather than other boys, are traditionally given brownie spirits is so that our families won't notice we are missing when we are off on brownie adventures.

"We most often attend school at private orphanages run by adult brownies who are our brownie sponsors, similar to your fairy mentors. The sponsors frequently arrange for us to be away doing brownie things, and sometimes they allow certain brownies to live in regular people's houses.

"The main reason feather duty is only six months at a time is because six months is long enough for any one brownie to be away from school." (Brownies were keepers of the Feather of Hope and had the important job of spreading hope all over the world.)

Most of the fairies had never heard that brownies were regular boys who were mostly orphans. They listened intently as Christopher went on with his story. "When brownies turn eighteen, they usually don't participate in very many brownie activities. Many of them go to college, like regular young men. Some get married and have families. Others just have careers. When grown, brownies are pretty much just like other people. Of course, it is in our nature to always enjoy mischief, but the urges to play tricks are slightly lessened as we age. For the most part, older brownies can control themselves properly to fit into society well enough.

"That is not to say that older brownies don't enjoy many of the same brownie games as they did in younger years. Even elderly brownies like sliding down curtains, stealing pickles, and blowing bubbles in people's houses to confuse them, since the people don't know where the bubbles are coming from."

Several of the fairies had started giggling at the description of the brownie antics, and Christopher smiled as he continued. "Also, some adult brownies still ride on animals. We can choose to do these things when we grow up, but most brownies just lead normal lives. Some return to help run the orphanages and teach.

"However, the leader of the brownies is always a younger brownie. I was chosen leader at age twelve. Brownies must always be led by one who still participates fully in all that is characteristic of brownies.

When I turn eighteen, a new leader will be chosen."

Christopher paused a moment before going on. "This brings me to another significant brownie fact concerning the few brownies who are not orphans. One particular family is blessed every generation with a male child who is given a brownie spirit. And each brownie in that family has made an extremely significant contribution to the brownie community throughout history.

"In the last century alone, Thomas, Patrick, Ernest, and Douglas have all accomplished great things. This family is considered to be brownie royalty.

"However," Christopher's voice took on a very solemn note as he continued, "the most recent brownie of this family was born sixty years ago. I am about to tell you the story of Prince Henry. Unfortunately, it is a sad tale, for the line of brownie princes stops with him."

29

Chapter Four

Henry and Rose

By now, all of the fairies were thoroughly engrossed in this interesting information about brownies. And they were especially excited to hear that there were brownie princes. The girls listened closely, hanging on Christopher's every word as he went on. "The story of Henry and Rose has to do with a wizard, a nymph, and a satyr. Prince Henry was a moss brownie. His significant contribution to brownie history was made just over forty years ago. He alone was able to convince Mother Nature that the brownies were responsible enough to carry the Feather of Hope.

"At age twenty, Henry was in college." Christopher paused slightly in his story to think. He blushed a little as he continued. "Henry was in love with a red rose fairy. Rose was also in college. They were planning to marry when they graduated. Forty years ago, people fell in love and married at slightly younger ages than they tend to now. Unfortunately, they were never able to marry.

"A powerful wizard named Victor Penchaant lived in a castle in a forest very near here. Victor was in love with a wood nymph named Amouril. Both Victor and Amouril foolishly trusted a satyr named Ribald who seemingly befriended them.

"The wizard and nymph lived some ways apart in the forest. Ribald did a lot of traveling and offered to carry messages back and forth between the two lovers.

Unknown to Victor and Amouril, the satyr was secretly in love with the enchanting nymph. Ribald often did not deliver their messages, as promised, though he would swear he had. This created confusion and suspicion between Victor and Amouril."

The fairies were all speechless, hanging on Christopher's every word as he went on with the story.

"One day, Amouril made her way close to Penchaant Castle. From a distance, she saw that Victor had company. A beautiful witch had come to stay with him. The visiting witch was actually Victor's sister. Amouril sent a message with Ribald to Victor, questioning if he still loved her and asking about his visitor. The satyr never delivered the message.

"Similarly, Victor sent a message to Amouril, telling her that he wanted her to come meet his sister, and asking why she had not answered his other messages.

Again, Ribald did not deliver the message. Not only that, but he also told Victor that Amouril said she never wanted to see him again. He then lied to the nymph, telling her that Victor fancied the witch and was planning to marry her.

"Heartbroken, Amouril left this area of the woods, wandered for years, and was never heard from again. As far as anyone knows, she is still out there. Tales are told by forest travelers, of seeing a weeping, wandering nymph; but no one has ever been able to get close enough to speak with her. And to this day, many beings do not trust satyrs because it is in their nature to stir up trouble and strife among others whenever they can."

At this point in the tale, the fairies were very saddened by what the mean satyr had done to the wizard and the nymph, and they were very anxious to hear how the story ended.

"Of course," continued Christopher, "Victor did not know of Ribald's deception. He was just very hurt and upset. How could his dearest love abandon him? In a fit of bitter rage, he enacted a dreadful curse on the first creatures he happened to see. Henry and Rose were on an outing in the woods, collecting fall leaves, very near Penchaant Castle. They were riding on a deer and enjoying the warm afternoon sun. Seeing their love and happiness, Victor cursed them with an irreversible curse." (The fairies gasped at this point in the story.)

"Rose is trapped in a painting inside the castle with only a bear cub for company. And Henry is imprisoned in a book with only an aardvark and a crow as companions. Neither can speak a word aloud, or leave the confines of the painting or book, or the other will die.

"Victor very much regretted unleashing this terrible fate on the young couple,

especially when he finally learned of Ribald's treachery. However, he could not undo his work," Christopher said sadly. "He contacted other fairies and brownies immediately. Then he consulted witches and elves in the hopes of finding some means of breaking the spell. So far, no magic has been discovered that can release them.

"Neither Henry nor Rose will age at all while they are trapped by the curse," Christopher added. "And the wizard made sure they have food and water. There is a table of food in the painting that magically refills itself. The bear cub fishes in a stream, and Rose collects berries from the hills beyond the stream in the painting. On the cover of the book, in the illustration, there is a picnic basket that always stays full. Plus, Henry can gather nuts, mushrooms, and seeds from the woods in the background of the picture in which he lives.

"The painting hangs in the main entry hall of Penchaant Castle. Henry's book is kept upstairs in the highest tower. It is too painful for Henry and Rose to be near enough to witness each other's imprisonment. That is why they are kept separate. Victor died several years ago, and the castle is not occupied. Henry and Rose live alone in that cold, empty fortress."

At this point in telling the story, Christopher paused for a very long time. There was a tear in his eye, which he tried to hide, and a choking lump in his throat. Several of the fairies were also crying. Jeffrey looked down and turned away. He was affected too, but he didn't cry, so he didn't want to embarrass Christopher by looking at him.

The entire fairy gathering was silent for some time, thinking about Henry and Rose and the wizard's sad tale.

Chapter Five

The Wishing Star

hristopher was able to continue talking a few minutes later after he had a couple sips of water. "Before the wizard died, he sent word to the fairies and brownies that there was a way to possibly break the spell.

"Once every seventy-two years, a certain wishing star appears. It is called the Wishing Star of Love, and it is visible for nine days only. The star is visible this week. It has the power, when wished upon, to lead the wisher to Paramour, the Goddess of Love, and her magic pearl, which is the tool she uses to grant wishes of love. Victor believed that her power would be capable of breaking the spell.

"The star is the only means to find the goddess," Christopher added. "She is well hidden, very secretive, and seldom grants wishes upon request. And Paramour can only be located at night because that is when she is awake. According to the legend of the star, if our wish to find the goddess is granted, a magical creature will come and take us to her. It is rumored that she often only grants wishes for love on a whim, just when she feels like it, so we must inspire her to help us."

Next, Madam Toad announced who would be embarking on this particular fairy mission. "I have decided that Moonflower, as our Fairy of Love, will lead this mission. Her ability to inspire passion may still be developing, but it will certainly be useful. Also, she has great storytelling

talents, which may be needed to persuade the fickle goddess to help. Rosemary, Primrose, and Luna will accompany her; and Madam Mariposa will supervise."

Primrose's real name was Taylor Buchanan. As a fairy, she wore a soft pink dress made of translucent flower petals with delicate gold veins. She also had tiny gold wings and shoulder-length, wavy blond hair. Her wand was a small, jet-black raven feather, and her fairy gift was the ability to solve mysteries by picking up on the smallest of clues. She loved reading mystery stories and was often able to figure out who the culprits were before any of the detectives even had a clue. It was easy to solve cases by looking at the details, such as the speck of mud on the windowsill, or the candle wax on the carpet, or the single red hair stuck to the shoe.

Hope Valdez was a luna moth fairy. She had straight dark hair and wore a glowing, soft green dress with matching slippers. Luna also had large, pale green wings with luminous eyespots, and her wand was a single thorn from a prickly pear cactus. However, Luna never used her wand and never needed to because one of her special fairy gifts was the ability to perform magic without a wand. She was the only fairy known to possess this gift. Luna also had amazing eyesight. She could see things clearly from long distances and could recognize things for what they really were. She was not often deceived by appearances. And like all moth fairies, she could perform well at night.

While backpacks were being readied for the fairies, Madam Toad explained why she had chosen this select fairy group. "Rosemary's memory will be very useful in helping Moonflower to recall the details of the story of Henry, Rose,

Victor, Amouril, and Ribald since it is somewhat complex. And since love is often a great mystery, Primrose may be needed to pick up on clues and offer suggestions. Also, Luna's night abilities and extraordinary eyesight will be helpful in searching for the Wishing Star of Love, especially since it may be cloudy tonight."

Then Madam Toad said, "Jeffrey and Christopher will escort you while you are traveling on this mission." Finally, the fairy leader bid the group farewell and wished them luck, adding, "Flitter forth fairies and take care of business!"

Provisions packed for the fairies included water, peanut butter and marshmallow crème sandwiches, raspberries, lemon jellybeans, powdered sugar puff pastries, blankets, pillows, and a star chart, also called a planisphere, indicating the position of the wishing star.

Out of curiosity, Moonflower and Luna looked up satyr in their fairy handbooks since they had never heard of a satyr before. This is the information that the handbooks shared:

> *Satyr: Satyrs are woodland creatures that are part man, part goat. Satyrs usually have the head and torso of a man with the two back legs of a goat. They are not very well liked by other magical creatures because satyrs enjoy causing problems. They are untrustworthy, often resorting to bribery, lies, and blackmail to get what they want. Satyrs can be very charming. However, their charm is part of the deception, and that type of behavior almost always means that they are up to no good. Fairies should avoid contact with satyrs if at all possible.*

Christopher had arranged for a jackrabbit to carry them to a position where they could best view the wishing star after darkness fell.

The rabbit approached the fairy gathering cautiously, sniffing the air as he took hesitant hops toward the trunk of the apricot tree. He was used to working with brownies, but he had never carried fairies before.

This was the largest rabbit any of the fairies had ever seen. Not only was he very tall; but also, his ears were as long, if not longer, than his body. Altogether, he was about three feet high, and this was a little intimidating to the tiny fairies. They waited quietly, huddled in a little group, not daring to go too near the giant rabbit by themselves.

Christopher noticed their apprehension and took charge. "Now this is a very nice jackrabbit, and very fast for traveling. But

47

you will need to climb onto him, rather than flying up to land on his back, because he is afraid of flying creatures."

"Even little fairies?" asked Moonflower.

"Yes, even little fairies," Christopher answered, smiling.

"But we couldn't hurt a rabbit," interjected Primrose. "He is a lot bigger than we are," she added, laughing.

Animals could understand fairies, especially in fairy form, because their voices were just the right tone and pitch to be heard clearly by animal ears. But even with hearing Primrose's words, the jackrabbit was looking fearfully at the fairies and was keeping his distance. His nose quivered and he crouched low to the ground as he watched them warily.

"Maybe it's the magic he doesn't like," said Rosemary. "That would be understandable. Even though none of us would hurt him, we could be capable of it." Then she added thoughtfully, wondering, "I hope no fairy has ever been mean to him or teased him."

"No, that's not it," answered Christopher. The brownie leader was helping Primrose adjust her backpack comfortably between her wings. As he tightened the shoulder strap for her, he added, "He is afraid of all flying creatures because when he was a little jackrabbit, a blue jay attacked him."

The fairies all looked sympathetically at the rabbit. Blue jays were often mean birds, and didn't much like other creatures.

"That makes sense then," said Luna. "Blue jays beat up on other birds and small animals all the time. They are often very cruel. I can see how they could be terrifying to a baby rabbit. Even big rabbits don't like blue jays because they're so fierce and scary."

"But that's not all," added Christopher. "Just as he was getting over the blue jay incident, he got himself into a nest of hornets. So now, he is scared of anything that flies." The jackrabbit was looking around him, as though keeping watch for blue jays and hornets.

The fairies, helped by Jeffrey and Christopher, climbed carefully onto the jackrabbit's back. They concentrated on not moving their wings and tried to keep them as still as possible so as not to startle or frighten the rabbit.

As she climbed up to the rabbit's shoulder, Moonflower spoke in the direction of one of his large ears. "None of us like hornets either. Yuck! They are just plain horrible. Even though they must serve some purpose in life, all they seem to do is buzz around and sting things."

The rabbit twitched his ears. He was happy to hear that someone else didn't like hornets either.

As the fairies were getting settled, Christopher told them, "You can hang onto his fur tightly if you need to; it won't hurt him." The fairies all grasped clumps of the silky fur firmly, and the jackrabbit took off with Christopher's urging.

This was the best ride any of the fairies had ever had. Christopher had been right—the jackrabbit was very fast. He loped through fields and woods, over hills and streams. It was a little bouncy but great fun for everyone, except Madam Mariposa who got somewhat motion sick.

"This would be a better ride for a spring chicken, rather than a grandmother fairy," she said.

"We could stop for a break," offered Jeffrey.

"No, I'm fine," she said. Then Madam Mariposa ate a lemon jellybean to try to settle her stomach. It worked. All fairies on the North American continent loved lemon jellybeans, but who would have thought they could cure nausea? This was certainly something new.

After several miles of loping, the jackrabbit came to a stop on the highest point of a hilltop clearing. Rows of trees rimmed the hilltop, but the immediate area was mostly clear. This would provide a perfect spot to view the wishing star after dark.

The jackrabbit sat down to allow the fairies to be closer to the ground, and they slid from his back, landing near his tail. Being careful to hold their wings still, the girls all went around to the front of the rabbit to thank him. The jackrabbit leaned his face down close to the fairies as each one of them thanked him graciously for the ride.

Moonflower patted the rabbit's nose. Then each of the other fairies followed suit, giving the velvety nose pats of thanks.

The jackrabbit's eyes squinted, his nose crinkled, and his whiskers twitched. It was pleasant, and kind of tickly, to have fairies pat his nose. *Some flying creatures are not bad after all*, he thought. *In fact, fairies are rather nice.* The rabbit's back foot thumped a bit as the fairies continued patting.

Christopher gave the rabbit a little scritch-scratch behind one ear as he said, "Thanks, I'll see you later." The rabbit playfully swatted Christopher with a swish of one giant ear. Christopher laughed as he was almost knocked over by the ear swipe. Then the jackrabbit was off as the fairies waved goodbye to him.

The fairies spread out their blankets on the grass and had a meal of peanut butter and marshmallow crème sandwiches, powdered sugar puff pastries, and raspberries, which they shared with the brownies. The brownies shared sunflower seeds and pecan pieces they had brought. Then everyone had lemon jellybeans for dessert and rested a little. They probably would not have a chance to sleep later, since they had to seek the goddess at night.

Just as the day was beginning to fade, Moonflower unpacked the star chart and studied the position of the Wishing Star of Love. The sky was somewhat cloudy, and she hoped the star would be visible. As the sun sank and darkness overtook the land, the fairies and brownies breathed a sigh of relief. Stars were visible, though faint.

Luna stood beside Moonflower to study the planisphere. Then she moved away from the others, her eyes scanning the sky.

After about fifteen minutes, she spotted the star. Though very tiny, it glowed and sparkled brightly with intense colors of red, gold, and purple. It truly was a magnificent sight. Luna pointed out the star to the others, who could see it, but were not able to distinguish the colors as well as she could.

Then Moonflower carefully and clearly made her wish. "I wish to find the Goddess Paramour." The others held their breaths, silently wishing the same thing Moonflower had just voiced.

For several minutes, nothing happened. Then the sky began to change, and lights from hundreds of stars began flashing brilliantly, in a specific order, forming a distinct outline in the dark heavens of space.

Rosemary gasped, as Primrose exclaimed in awe, "The stars form the shape of a unicorn! A unicorn!"

"Yes," said Luna softly. "A unicorn."

But Luna wasn't looking up. Her gaze was fixed at a point on the ground in the distance, near one of the trees that ringed the hilltop.

The rest of the group was speechless as a brilliant white unicorn galloped up to them. He was so bright and radiant that they almost felt the need to look away. However, none of them could draw their watering eyes from the beautiful creature. His sparkling coat gleamed like fresh snow in the pale starlight, and his tail and mane fluttered in rippling waves with the soft evening breezes.

Finally, Primrose was able to speak, and she whispered, "This is more exciting than any mystery."

"This must be the magical creature that will take us to the goddess," Moonflower added.

As if in answer, the unicorn bowed his noble head slowly and lowered his golden horn to the ground so the brownies could climb onto his head. The horn was very warm and felt alive with a tingly vibration, as though it contained some great energy.

The fairies all flew up to the magnificent head and sat behind Christopher and Jeffrey on the unicorn's neck, grasping his mane to be secure for the ride.

But there was really no need to hang on. They weren't bounced at all as the unicorn started off, first at a trot, then accelerating to a gallop. Though they must have been traveling very fast, the brownies and fairies felt no movement at all. Soon, the scenery was whizzing by them so quickly that it made them dizzy. But it was as though they were sitting very still, like on an unmoving carousel horse.

Chapter Six

Paramour and the Pearl of Love

he unicorn took them deep into a tangled forest, and deeper still into darkness. Except for the faint glint of stars occasionally visible through the dense, over-hanging tree limbs, there was very little light in the forest. Moonflower, Luna, and the unicorn glowed softly, but not enough to dispel the eerie feel of the dark surroundings.

Moonflower and Rosemary took out their wands and whispered, "*Fairy light*," causing the tips of the icicle and braided orangutan hairs to glow. The extra light seemed to lift some of the spookiness from the air.

While they traveled, Primrose looked up unicorns in her fairy handbook and read the entry aloud to her friends:

"*Unicorns:* *Unicorns resemble horses and are usually pure white with a single horn extending from their foreheads. They are largely mysterious magical creatures because it is unknown what the unicorns' exact purposes are or how far their magical abilities extend. It is known that unicorns are attracted to apple trees. They also have the ability to give direction, guidance, and advisement to other creatures by mere thought since they cannot speak. Their advice is valuable because unicorns are pure creatures and cannot be corrupted. Unicorn wisdom is entirely unbiased, containing no ulterior*

motives or prejudices. It is said that unicorns can never be captured. However, an old legend disputes this, stating that unicorns are susceptible to capture by beautiful maidens such as nymphs."

After many miles, the unicorn stopped by a large pile of boulders sitting next to a steep rock cliff. In the dim light, the fairies could see a narrow opening between two of the rocks that led to the mouth of a cave. The cave entrance was barely visible, hidden by clever, overlapping placement of the boulders. As the unicorn again lowered his head, the fairies and brownies dismounted. They thanked the unicorn, and he left quickly with a soft snort and a swish of his flowing, snowy-white tail.

The group made their way cautiously to the entrance of the cave. As they stepped

Unicorns:
Unicorns resemble horses and are usually pure white with a single horn extending from their foreheads.

in a few feet, a soft light beckoned them from farther in. As they moved forward, the cave opened into a large chamber, softly lit by a single object: a magnificent, glowing pearl as large as a grapefruit.

The lustrous white pearl was sitting on a blue satin cloth in the middle of a marble pedestal near the center of the chamber. The pearl gave off a ghostly light that made everything in the room gleam with soft halos.

The other furnishings in the cave were very ornate and elaborate. There were fancy throws, rugs, and tapestries with detailed needlework designs. Sculpted chairs, poufs, and divans were placed throughout the room, covered with elegant cloth in rich colors like harvest gold, royal purple, and emerald green.

There was also an assortment of intricately wrought chests and boxes. Many artistic samples of pottery, silver, and blown glass sat on corner shelves and raised platforms throughout the chamber. And multitudes of paintings covered the walls, depicting scenes of nature and couples in love—walking hand in hand, sitting quietly together, and embracing one another.

As the fairies and brownies were taking all of this in, the Goddess of Love entered the main cave chamber from a small side passageway. She was as pale as the pearl itself and wore an elegant, gauzy white dress that shimmered with light.

The goddess' hair was very long, and so blond that it was nearly white. It lay in soft ringlets down her back and over her shoulders. Her eyes were a very pale, clear blue, and she carried a single, pure white peacock feather.

When the goddess spoke, her lilting voice was full of warmth and laughter, like a babbling brook on a spring morning. "Welcome, fairies and brownies. I am

65

the Goddess of Paramour

Paramour, Goddess of Love. You are my first visitors in seventy-two years. The Wishing Star of Love must be doing its job tonight."

Moonflower stepped forward, nodding. "Yes," she said, "we sought out the star and wished to find you. We are seeking your help to right a terrible wrong in order to unite two young lovers separated for forty years."

The goddess was smiling, but serious, as she responded. "I don't very often grant requests. I travel the earth with the pearl, bestowing love by my own judgment. You will need to convince me that your cause is worthy. But I must warn you that I have heard many sorrowful tales of lost love, and very few of them have inspired me to use my power to change their circumstances. The world is filled with love, and people must make their own choices and live with the consequences."

The fairies and brownies were invited to take seats on a ginger-colored velvet chair while the goddess lounged on a ruby-red satin divan.

Moonflower then took a deep breath and began to tell the story of Henry, Rose, Victor, Amouril, and Ribald.

Occasionally, she paused to think; and twice, Rosemary whispered in her ear to remind her of key events. Whenever she could, Moonflower embellished the story to include many details that would make the characters more real and sympathetic. Truly, she *was* a master storyteller. She stressed the point that Henry and Rose were completely innocent in the whole affair, and did not contribute in any way to their terrible fate. They were simply in the wrong place at the wrong time.

Moonflower also made a point of telling the goddess that while the wizard eventually discovered the satyr's deception, the nymph never learned the truth, and to this day, wanders the woods, weeping for lost love, still hurting from what she believes was betrayal.

Finally, Moonflower stressed that Victor himself, so regretful of having caused Henry and Rose such misery, had continued to seek a means to break the curse right up to his dying day. It had been the wizard's own idea to seek the Wishing Star of Love and to request Paramour's help.

When she finished speaking, the other fairies were weeping softly with the sadness of her story, so beautifully told. Even Jeffrey and Christopher were sniffling.

The goddess, however, just looked casually amused, and she had a small smile on her face. With a slight wave of her white peacock feather, tiny silk handkerchiefs appeared in front of the fairies and brownies, each embroidered with a small *P* in the corner.

After the tears and sniffles subsided, the goddess spoke. "That is truly a beautiful tale, and very sad. I clearly understand the innocence of Henry, Rose, and Amouril. Victor is also largely innocent, though it would have been much better if he had been able to control his temper. Wizards and witches should know better. They are expected to follow many of the same guide-lines of other magical creatures, and are not allowed to abuse their powers. Having otherwise only been guilty of trusting unwisely, I cannot deny helping you to fix his mistake. However, the mission to break the spell will not be an easy one. I can give you the tool needed to accomplish the task, but you will have to carry it out."

The goddess then rose from her divan and approached the pearl. With another wave of the white peacock feather, the pearl

glowed more brightly and began to hum with a kind of slow, haunting music. As the goddess closed her eyes, the humming grew louder.

Suddenly, a beam of pale blue light shot from the pearl. Across the room, exactly where the beam of light bounced off the wall, a small white candle appeared floating in the air, lit with an icy blue flame.

Chapter Seven

The Candle of Inamorata

"I have summoned the Candle of Inamorata," said Paramour. "It is the only thing powerful enough to break the curse. You must carry the candle to Castle Penchaant without allowing the flame to go out. The candle will burn until sunset tomorrow, at which time, it will extinguish. Before that time, Henry and Rose must both be brought together to blow out the candle. They must do this simultaneously, at exactly the same moment, for the magic to work properly in order to lift the spell."

Moonflower nodded her understanding.

The goddess retrieved the floating candle from its hovering spot in midair and handed it to Moonflower, who took it carefully with both hands. It was not much larger than a birthday cake candle so she was able to hold it easily.

Smiling, Paramour gave her final words of advice. "Be careful of wind and water," the goddess warned. "The candle will be useless if it goes out. Castle Penchaant is several miles from here, so you will need to leave very early in the morning to reach the fortress in time to break the spell before sunset."

The fairies and brownies were invited to stay in the cave for the rest of the night. It would have been unwise to leave on their journey at night. For one thing, it was very windy outside the cave. And they would not have been able to travel in darkness safely through the forest by themselves.

Moonflower carefully propped the candle up with several small stones. Then they all got out their blankets and pillows and went to bed. Tiredness, along with Rosemary's piney-minty fragrance and the mesmerizing glow of the pearl, soon lulled them all into a deep sleep.

Paramour woke them before dawn. "I am asleep during daylight," she told them, "so I need to bid you farewell before the sun rises. Goodbye and good luck."

The fairies and brownies were thankful to be wakened early so they could get started on the long trek to the castle. As the group set off carefully with the candle, they were also happy that the morning was still and quiet.

In the daylight, the woods looked very different. Christopher and Jeffrey, who were very familiar with this region of the forest, recognized their surroundings and knew which direction to travel to seek the castle.

They took turns carrying the candle. The clear blue flame gave off no warmth, but burned steadily, hardly ever wavering.

As they walked, Christopher speculated, "I wonder if we could cover the candle somehow to protect it. Then we could travel on birds to reach the castle more quickly."

"I don't think we can cover it," said Luna.

"She's right," added Primrose. "Fire needs oxygen."

"And it might be dangerous to try a protective spell too near it," said Moonflower, glancing at her grandmother.

Madam Mariposa was nodding. "Since we don't know much about the candle, it would not be wise to attempt any magic close to it."

After several hours of walking, the travelers rested and ate a small lunch of peanut butter and marshmallow crème sandwiches, raspberries, and sunflower seeds.

As they ate, Moonflower asked Christopher and Jeffrey a rather personal question. "Since we are on a mission of love, I have been wondering, do either of you have a girlfriend?"

Jeffrey turned bright red, and Christopher looked up at her, surprised. The other young fairies' mouths dropped open. They couldn't believe Moonflower had asked the brownies this question. Madam Mariposa just smiled and looked away.

In an effort to break the tension, Moonflower spoke again to try to explain herself. "None of us have boyfriends because we're too young. But since you are both older, I just wondered if you had girlfriends. You know, because our mission is kind of related to that."

Jeffrey shook his head and spoke first, still red. "No, I don't have a girlfriend right now."

Christopher cleared his throat before he answered. "Well, I am friends with Milkweed of the far North region. Her name is Caitlin. We are not really boyfriend and girlfriend, but we are hoping to go to the same college. Maybe…someday…." His words trailed off and he looked down shyly. Not many people knew that he liked Milkweed.

No one said anything else about this matter, and they finished eating in silence.

The group had a slight panic episode after lunch when it started to drizzle. Thinking quickly, Rosemary grabbed a large, dried sycamore leaf and held it over the candle. Jeffrey did the same thing on the other side of the candle.

Together, he and Rosemary formed a pretty good, sycamore-leaf-umbrella to protect the flame. Thank goodness the drizzle never turned to rain.

The fairies and brownies walked as quickly as they could but started to worry in the afternoon.

"We are still about two miles from the castle," fretted Christopher, "and the days are short this time of year."

"Even if we fly slowly, we will create a breeze," said Luna. "So what should we do?"

Jeffrey had been thinking very hard on the matter since lunchtime. "What about a fox?" he suggested. "Foxes can walk fairly slowly, but still faster than we can, and they don't bounce around as much as squirrels or rabbits."

"What a good idea," said Christopher. Next, both he and Jeffrey suddenly gave wild cries and whistles that sounded like

strange bird calls in an effort to attract a fox. The fairies were very surprised at the extremely loud noises coming from the rather small brownies. Fairies couldn't make that much noise even if they tried.

Three squirrels and a hawk arrived first, and were sent away by the brownies. Finally, a gray fox appeared in answer to the brownies' calls. Jeffrey explained that they needed to travel, but slowly, and the fox nodded his understanding.

Carefully holding the candle as still as possible, Moonflower slowly flew up to the shoulder area of the fox. The other fairies followed suit, and the brownies climbed up his leg.

The fox was indeed very careful about walking slowly; the flame barely flickered as he plodded along through the forest.

Chapter Eight

Castle Penchaant and the Twisted Staircase

arly evening, about an hour before dark, the group finally came upon the castle.

Castle Penchaant was an extremely tall fortress, but not very wide. And the structure was spindly, like a slender arm reaching for the sky. The turreted towers were barely visible as they poked their sharp roof-tips into the low-hanging puffy clouds shrouding them. Christopher explained that the castle was not visible to regular human beings because it was magically disguised to look like tall rock spires.

As they approached the front door, the fairies noticed that exactly half of the castle was covered with climbing red roses. The other half was covered by thick green moss. Jeffrey told the fairies that the roses bloomed year round, and the moss also flourished, no matter what time of year it was or what the weather was like.

An unusual sight greeted the fairies as they entered the castle. A broom and dustpan were hard at work, by themselves, at the far end of the entry hall. The broom was sweeping up clouds of dust, and the dustpan was trying very hard to catch the billowing dirt.

Both of these bewitched objects completely ignored the visitors. Christopher and Jeffrey had been to the castle before and knew about the magic broom and dustpan, so they weren't surprised. They smiled at the startled looks of amusement on the fairies' faces.

At a small side table in the entry, a lambswool duster was floating in midair, making lazy swipes at the surface of the dusty table. When the duster noticed the fairies, it gave a small gasp, then began furiously dusting the table and a nearby lamp, as if trying to spiff up the castle for the visitors.

The painting that was Rose's home was very prominent and easy to spot on the wall by the foot of an enormous spiraled staircase. Rose was sitting in the grass eating an apple under a small tree in the forefront of the painting, and the bear cub was splashing about in the stream looking for fish.

When Rose noticed the visitors, she stood up and waved. She recognized the brownies. The brownies and fairies all waved back. Rose had dark curly hair and tiny scarlet wings. Her rose petal dress was the exact, deep red color of the climbing

roses outside the castle. The dress came to just below her knees, and she had soft slippers to match.

Realizing that they were running out of time, Moonflower took charge. "How are we going to get Henry and Rose together to blow out the candle at the same time?" she asked.

Rosemary and Primrose both spoke at once, but had different thoughts: "We should take the painting upstairs to the book," said Rosemary, while Primrose voiced at exactly the same time, "We should bring the book down to the painting."

Rosemary quickly acknowledged that Primrose had the better idea. "You're right," she said. "It would be much easier to bring the book to the painting, rather than the other way round."

Moonflower quickly handed the candle to Christopher, who stayed by the painting with Jeffrey and Madam Mariposa to explain to Rose what needed to happen. Then Rosemary, Luna, Primrose, and Moonflower began the long journey up the twisted staircase to retrieve the book from the highest tower.

Even though they were flying, it seemed they would never reach the top. In truth, Castle Penchaant had thirty-three floors. It was built practically straight up with very few hallways since the castle wasn't at all wide. When the fairies finally reached the uppermost level, they easily found the small turret room that contained the book, which was propped up on a short round table beside an armchair.

Henry noticed the fairies immediately. The brownie prince was dressed in dark green clothes and had a moss cap covering his light brown hair. The aardvark was standing beside him in the long field grass, and the crow was perched on a barren tree limb.

As the fairies neared the book, Henry quickly held up several pieces of paper. He had evidently torn words from the pages of the book to be able to communicate with visitors.

Four times, in rapid succession, Henry lifted words for them to see. The message read, "can't Leave book or speak or friend Will die."

"We know! We know!" said Moonflower hastily. "We need to get you downstairs. There's a way to break the spell."

Henry braced himself against the tree trunk as the four fairies each grabbed a corner of the book. It was very heavy. They were all struggling by the time they reached the staircase. Moonflower was silently wondering how they were going to manage the long descent, when Luna had a brilliant idea. "The banister is very

polished and smooth," she said. "If we slide the book down the railing, balancing it, we will reach the bottom faster."

The fairies balanced the book on the stair railing, each of them carefully holding a corner.

"Hang on!" Rosemary told Henry.

Henry sat with his back to the tree trunk, holding tightly to the aardvark, while the crow dug his claws into the tree branch.

The trip down was a little unsteady but was indeed, as Luna predicted, very fast. The book wavered and tipped, but the fairies never lost hold of it. However, they weren't able to fly fast enough to keep up with the sliding book that was gathering speed as it slid down the slippery spiral rail. Within a few seconds, the fairies were being pulled so fast that their feet sailed behind them, as though they were riding on a toboggan.

At the very bottom, the book hit the finial of the stair banister with a hard bump, jarring the occupants. But Henry and his friends were not harmed—just a bit shook up.

They were only just in time. The sun was still visible, but barely. As it began to set, the hall turned a dusky pinkish-gray color. As quickly as they could, the fairies carried the heavy book to a position facing the painting. Then they hurriedly told Henry what he needed to do.

Rosemary, Luna, and Primrose held the book firmly while hovering as close as possible to the painting. Moonflower retrieved the candle from Christopher and flew into position, holding it steadily between Henry and Rose. "On the count of three," she said. "One, Two, Three, *BLOW!*"

The icy blue flame was extinguished instantly as Henry and Rose blew together as hard as they could. For a moment, nothing happened. Then the Candle of Inamorata simply disappeared at the same moment the sun's final golden-pink ray slipped away to sleep for the night.

With the disappearance of the candle, the fairies and brownies were left standing and wondering. Rose and Henry looked at each other fondly, but neither spoke nor tried to exit their forty-year homes. They were afraid to test whether the spell had actually been broken.

The fairies placed the book on the floor so that Henry could step out. Still, he hesitated.

"Love is about taking chances," said Moonflower suddenly, startling everyone in the room. "You will have to risk it," she added.

Henry smiled and nodded, then confidently stepped from the cover of the book to the stone floor. Looking up at Rose a moment later, he found her perfectly healthy.

Christopher, Jeffrey, and Madam Mariposa breathed a sigh of relief and laughed, while the young fairies clapped their hands and giggled happily.

Rose had left the painting and was speedily flying down to hug Henry. He held her tightly and finally spoke. "Oh, how I have missed you." Rose was not yet able to speak. She wept silently on Henry's shoulder as he placed a soft kiss on the top of her head.

The fairies carefully carried Henry's book up to the freshly dusted hall table so that it would be off of the floor. The crow cawed happily, while the aardvark rolled around in the grass. In the painting, the bear cub got so excited that he bounded in circles, upsetting the table of food. They were all rejoicing for their friends.

Rose was finally able to find her voice a few moments later. With tears still streaming down her cheeks, she faced the visitors. "Thank you," she said softly.

Outside the castle, Christopher and Jeffrey called a hawk and a falcon to take them all home. Henry and Rose joined them, hand in hand, to say goodbye.

The moonlight and starlight were just bright enough for the fairies and brownies to realize that a most amazing change had taken place outside of the castle. The moss and climbing roses had intertwined, and were now laced together over the walls of the fortress.

Henry told them, "The wizard left the castle to us so we have a place to live. And, naturally, we want to live here, to stay

close to the book and painting, to keep company with our longtime friends."

As the hawk and falcon were just taking off, Rose called to the fairies and brownies. "You will all be invited to our wedding!"

Back at home the following week, Moonflower received a nut message from Christopher, thanking her for her help. He also told her that the Goddess Paramour had somehow contacted Amouril and told her the truth about the satyr's deception and Victor's true devotion to her. And Henry and Rose, on one of their evening walks around the castle grounds, had actually seen the beautiful nymph from a distance, laying flowers on Victor Penchaant's grave.

The End

Fairy Fun

Cook or bake your way into someone's heart.

Fairy Fudge
(Courtesy of Madam Mariposa)

3 C. sugar
³/₄ C. evaporated milk
1 stick butter or margarine
7 oz. jar marshmallow créme
12 oz. pkg. semi-sweet chocolate chips
1 t. vanilla

Combine sugar, milk, and butter in medium saucepan. Bring to full boil over moderate heat, stirring frequently. Boil for 5 minutes, stirring occasionally.

Remove from heat. Add other ingredients. Stir until chocolate is melted and pour into greased 9 x 13 cake pan. Allow to cool, then cut into pieces of any size. The fairies like three-bite pieces. Fudge is wonderful either at room temperature or refrigerated.

You can add nuts, if desired, or use peanut butter baking chips instead of chocolate for Peanut Butter Fairy Fudge. If adding nuts, do so at the time the chocolate chips are added.

Be sure to get permission from your parents to cook in the kitchen, and make sure a grown up helps when using sharp instruments and hot appliances.

Sundials

While you may or may not be able to find the Wishing Star at this particular time of year, there is a very special star you can easily find during the day—the sun! The sun is a very powerful and very important star to us: it gives us light, heat, energy, and keeps the earth in its orbit. The sun can even help you tell what time it is. By making a simple sundial, you can tell the time wherever you go without a watch.

You will need:
    A piece of cardboard or stiff paper
    A drinking straw or pencil
    Tape
    A pen or pencil to write with
    A compass
    A watch (to set up the sundial)

On a sunny day, find an open spot on the ground where your sundial will not be blocked by any shade. Place the cardboard flat on the ground and poke a hole through the center (you may need an adult's help with this part). Push the drinking straw (or pencil) through the center of the hole so that it is standing straight up (perpendicular) from the cardboard. Use the tape to secure the straw to the cardboard.

At the top of the piece of cardboard, write the number "12" just like on the top of a clock. Use your compass to determine where north is and put the number "12" in that exact direction. Look at your watch to see what time it is. Wherever the sun's shadow is on the cardboard, make a mark to show it is that time. For example, if it is 1:00, put a "1" on the cardboard where the shadow is.

Check back at different times of the day and continue marking numbers where the shadow is on the cardboard for those times. Once you have all the numbers, 1 through 12, on the sundial, you can take it inside and decorate it! Whenever you want to use it again, just point the 12 toward north and you will always be able to tell time without your watch.

FAIRY FACTS

Unicorns of Yesterday and Today

Though many stories and artwork of today feature unicorns that resemble horses with a single horn, the unicorns of old looked much different. Many traditional unicorns of legend had cloven hooves, beards like goats, and lions' tails. Variations included a one-horned sea creature and a land animal with feet like an elephant and a tail like a pig. Some of these descriptions may have been based on sightings of real creatures such as narwhal and rhinoceros. Based on human fascination and numerous stories, both old and new, whatever their appearances, unicorns will always symbolize power, solitude, beauty, purity, and mystery.

Valentine's Day

On February fourteenth each year, people all over the world celebrate Valentine's Day in various ways, often by exchanging notes, flowers, candy, and other gifts with those they love. Pairs of lovebirds, which are small parrots, are symbolic of this holiday. Other symbols of Valentine's Day include heart-shaped items, such as cards and candy boxes, and images of Cupid with his bow and arrow. It is said that anyone hit by one of Cupid's arrows will fall madly in love with the next person he or she sees.

Primrose and the Magic Snowglobe

Burchard the gargoyle has just been fired from his job guarding a church from evil spirits because he can't stop walking around, Ripper the gremlin is fixing things instead of breaking them, and Mr. Jones the dwarf is telling people his own name and spreading dwarf secrets to non-dwarves. What is wrong with these people?

When Madam Toad had everyone's attention, she spoke more solemnly. "By now, many of you may have guessed why our visitors are here. It is unusual for a gargoyle to move around, for a gremlin to enjoy fixing things, and for a dwarf to reveal secrets. As far as anyone can tell, these are recent and singular occurrences among gargoyles, gremlins, and dwarves. Burchard has been fired from his job. Ripper has been driven out and is being pursued by other gremlins. And Mr. Jones has been banished by the dwarves.

"We have no idea how these things occurred," Madam Toad continued, "and a reason why must be found so that things can be put to right."

Primrose, Luna, and Snapdragon are put on the case, with the help of Madam Swallowtail. Interestingly, all three of the magical creatures remember making a wish and seeing a man with a snowglobe. Could it really be that the Wishmaker has returned? Primrose must use her detective abilities to solve the mystery.

Come visit us at fairychronicles.com

Luna and the Well of Secrets

Luna and the Well of Secrets

J. H. SWEET

Three bat fairies have been kidnapped and taken to the Well of Secrets. To make matters worse, the Well of Secrets is the doorway to Eventide, the Land of Darkness!

"There must be extremely powerful magic involved to snatch fairies from three completely different parts of the world all in one day."

Madam Toad's face wore a puzzled expression as she continued. "And the reason only bat fairies were abducted is unknown..."

Luna, Snapdragon, Firefly, and Madam Finch are sent to the Well to discover why. Once there, they discover a Dark Witch imprisoned in a mirror, only able to come out for twelve minutes every twelve hours. Then a Light Witch arrives and the fairies have to make a choice. Who do they trust? Which one is good and which one is evil? Will they defeat the right witch without destroying the balance between light and dark?

This may be the most dangerous fairy mission ever!

Come visit us at fairychronicles.com

Dewberry and the Lost Chest of Paragon

In Dewberry's constant quest to obtain more knowledge, she uncovers the Legend of Paragon, an ancient ruler, and his three marshals— Exemplar, Criterion, and Apotheosis. Dewberry enlists the aid of her friends, Primrose and Snapdragon, in seeking the Lost Chest of Paragon, rumored to contain a great gift of ancient and powerful knowledge, one she hopes to share with all of mankind.

"Maybe it's a cure for cancer," suggested Primrose.

"Or diabetes, or epilepsy, or cystic fibrosis," added Snapdragon hopefully.

Primrose had another idea. "Maybe it's a blueprint for World Peace," she said.

The girls were very excited about the many possibilities.

But when the chest is found, a catastrophe occurs, one so powerful that even fairy magic is nowhere near strong enough to fix the problem. But it was Dewberry's relentless search for knowledge that caused this disaster in the first place. She will have to do everything she can to make it right again...

Come visit us at fairychronicles.com

Élan the dragon must complete the Rites of Dragondom to earn the respect of his fellow dragons and pass into adulthood. In order to do this, he has to face off with four dangerous monsters. But Élan is not a violent dragon and he needs the fairies' help!

"My odyssey involves a quest to obtain a fabulous jewel for my queen. I must get past the four monsters, obtain the jewel, and return with it to Queen Elektra; and I have to complete this journey all in one day. The path of the quest is very widespread, covering much distance. But that is not a problem... the problem is that I do not want to hurt any of the creatures I must face. They are terrible foes, and many dragons would likely just plow them down... but it is against my nature to harm others. I need to successfully complete my challenge, but I must somehow find a way to do it without hurting others so that I can still live with myself afterwards. For me, the journey is not as simple as obtaining the jewel for my queen. That would actually be quite an easy task. With force, it would be easy for any dragon to just take what he wants. This is more a test of my true character. And I want to do what is right, rather than what is easy."

Snapdragon, Dove, and Madam Swallowtail will join Élan on this quest. But Élan's plan to avoid hurting others is a difficult one as the fairies must get past four very dangerous monsters that are ready to fight!

Come visit us at fairychronicles.com

Harlequin and the Pebble of Spree

The Spirit of Fun and Frolic, responsible for spreading happiness, is in trouble. If the Pebble of Spree is not found soon, the world will suffer from a lack of happiness!

"We have come to help you," Harlequin said gently. "Please, tell us what is wrong so that we can try to fix the problem."

Still crying, but with slightly less sobbing, the spirit choked out, "I have a *h-h*-hole in *m*-my heart. The only thing that can *f-f*-fix it is the *P*-Pebble of Spree." With these few words, the crying subsided slightly further, and the spirit was able to go on without excessive tears. "The Pebble of Spree is in the brook," she said softly.

The spirit pointed a short ways downstream, sniffing a little as she went on. "But it must somehow be retrieved without anyone touching the water. The pebble is the only thing that can heal the hole in my heart. If you can find some way to obtain it, I can go on with my job of spreading happiness. Otherwise, I will waste away with grief."

Harlequin is the good-natured fairy of jokes and mischief. Together with her friends—Dove, Cricket, and Blue (a blue dragonfly fairy)—she must retrieve the Pebble of Spree. But Harlequin quickly discovers that it will take the help of many others to complete this mission!

Come visit us at fairychronicles.com

The adventures don't end here!

Come visit us at
www.fairychronicles.com

for even more fairy magic and fun!

- Become a Fairy Chronicles member
- Upload your own fairy drawings
- Read about all of the *Fairy Chronicles* adventures—and get sneak peeks of the next books
- Meet each fairy and learn more about your favorite characters
- Help protect Mother Nature with cool recycling activities and ideas
- Check out the online Fairy Handbook as well as trivia, recipes, poems, and crafts
- Download special bookmarks, computer graphics, and more free stuff
- Send your friends *Fairy Chronicles* e-cards

And much more!

About the Author

J.H. Sweet has always looked for the magic in the everyday. She has an imaginary dog named Jellybean Ebenezer Beast. Her hobbies include hiking, photography, knitting, and basketry. She also enjoys watching a variety of movies and sports. Her favorite superhero is her husband, with Silver Surfer coming in a close second. She loves many of the same things the fairies love, including live oak trees, mockingbirds, weathered terra-cotta, butterflies, bees, and cypress knees. In the fairy game of "If I were a jellybean, what flavor would I be?" she would be green apple. J.H. Sweet lives with her husband in South Texas and has a degree in English from Texas State University.

About the Illustrator

Holly Sierra's illustrations are visually enchanting with particular attention to decorative, mystical, and multicultural themes. Holly received her fine arts education at SUNY Purchase in New York and lives in Myrtle Beach with her husband, Steve, and their three children, Gabrielle, Esme, and Christopher.